This book

Contents

c| 2158992

Ladybird

Cover illustration by Paula Martyr
Text pages 31-32 by Judith Nicholls (© MCMXCVII)

Published by Ladybird Books Ltd
80 Strand, London WC2R 0RL
A Penguin Company

4 6 8 10 9 7 5

© LADYBIRD BOOKS LTD MCMXCVII, MMI

Printed in Italy

Monster
haircut!

written by Marie Birkinshaw

illustrated by Paula Martyr

Mum looked at Gemma.
"Your hair's too long,"
Mum said. "It's time you
went to the hairdressers'."

"Oh, no," said Gemma.

"Oh, yes," said Mum.
"I'll call Sandra to see if
she can do it."

Gemma pulled a face.

"Oh, Mum! Can't we go somewhere new? Sandra's so boring," she said.

So Mum took Gemma
to the new hairdressers'
in town.

Gemma sat down.
A weird hairdresser put
a gown round her neck.

Gemma pulled a face.

"Would Madam like green hair?" the hairdresser asked.

Just then another hairdresser came running over. "Oh, no!" he said.

"Green wouldn't be right at all. I think pink and yellow would look much better."

Gemma pulled a face.

"Who wants to look like that?" she said. "Come on, Mum! Let's go to Sandra's."

The hairdressers pulled faces
at one another!

"Oh, no! Don't go to Sandra's,"
they said. "She's so boring!"

Who am I?

written by Shirley Jackson

illustrated by Allan Wittert

My first is in wall,
but it isn't in ball.

My second is in dog,
but it isn't in dig.

My third is in bear,
but it isn't in bean.

My fourth is in mouse,
but it isn't in house.

Who am I?

Worm!

Looking for gold

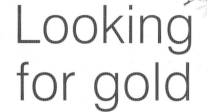

written by Marie Birkinshaw
illustrated by Pauline King

Dad was in the garden.
I was helping him
to put up a fence.

Dad asked, "Do you think
we'll find some gold
in this hole?"

I said, "I don't know.
Let's have a look!"

In went the spade.

We found

a spider,

a beetle,

lots of worms

and some soil.

In went the spade again.
This time we found

a bird's feather,

some little pebbles,

a snail's shell

and more soil.

The spade went in again,
and we found some black
rock, an old broken pot
and lots more soil!

I was getting bored.
"Isn't that hole big enough?"
I asked.

"Just one more spadeful,"
said Dad.

Then his spade hit…

GOLD!

Soil Facts

- Soil is the loose covering of broken rocks and decaying material that covers the rock around the Earth's surface.

- Some of the creatures that live in the soil are called *decomposers*. These include worms, bacteria, fungi and algae. They eat the remains of dead plants and animals, and help to improve the soil.

- A teaspoonful of soil may contain billions of different bacteria.

- About 10 tonnes of soil can pass through the average worm each year. The waste soil is sometimes passed to the surface as worm casts. This can raise the surface of the soil by about 15–20cms every 100 years. Worm burrows help to break up the soil, allowing in air and water.

Soil settles into different levels. Each level contains particular things that make up soil.

Leaf litter and other decaying plants and animals.

Topsoil – a dark and fertile layer of soil where most of the decomposers live.

Subsoil – richer, older soil where deep tree roots grow.

Weathered rock – broken pieces of bedrock.

Bedrock – solid rock at the Earth's surface.

The spider's walk

written by Judith Nicholls

illustrated by David Mostyn

There's a big, hairy spider,
Climbing the door.

Here's a big, hairy spider,
Back on the floor.

There's a big, hairy spider,

Creeping to you.

Nearer and nearer,
  nearer and nearer.

Here's a big, hairy spider…

What will you do?

RUN!

The spider's walk

Help your child with any words he cannot read,
and then have fun reading this rhyme faster
and faster – with dramatic actions.

New words

Encourage your child to use some of these new words
to help him to write his own very simple stories and
rhymes. Go back to look at earlier books and their
wordlists to practise other words. The Soil Facts are
for you to share with your child to motivate him to
find out more. Vocabulary used is
not included in the list of
new words.

Read with Ladybird

Read with Ladybird has been written to help you to help your child:

- to take the first steps in reading
- to improve early reading progress
- to gain confidence

Main Features

- **Several stories and rhymes in each book**

This means that there is not too much for you and your child to read in one go.

- **Rhyme and rhythm**

Read with Ladybird uses rhymes or stories with a rhythm to help your child to predict and memorise new words.

- **Gradual introduction and repetition of key words**

Read with Ladybird introduces and repeats the 100 most frequently used words in the English language.

- **Compatible with school reading schemes**

The key words that your child will learn are compatible with the word lists that are used in schools. This means that you can be confident that practising at home will support work done at school.

- **Information pullout**

Use this pullout to understand more about how you can use each story to help your child to learn to read.

But the most important feature of **Read with Ladybird** is for you and your child to have fun sharing the stories and rhymes with each other.